Pinky and Bird

Dr. Claudia Nicholson

Illustrations by
Jagath Kosmodara

Brer Anancy Press

First Edition
ISBN: 978-9768266170

Ordering Information:
Quantity sales. Special discounts are available on quantity purchases by corporations, associations, and others.

For details, contact:
Brer Anancy Press
3701 W. Santa Rosalia Dr.
Los Angeles, CA 90008
info@breranancypress.com
www.BrerAnancyPress.com

Printed in the United States of America

THIS BOOK BELONGS TO

____

A CR-A-ZY King Charles Spaniel
lies in the washing clothes,
And why they call her Pinky
it's how the story goes…

The truth be told as tails would go
it won't take a while to see,
How this cute and furry doggy
was NAUGHTY as can be.

It all began one day in may
when looking for a home,
Pinky and Bird and Mum and Dad
found a CASTLE they could own.

The rooms were many and stairwells three
the view far as could be,
Happily they sat on the balcony
all were looking out to SEA.

From top to tail and paws of four
they must find a place to keep,
The problem lay in PINKY'S SNORE
where could they all but sleep?

Brother Bird, first of the herd
was truly undeterred,
Why he could not be consoled
and sleep like the days of OLD.

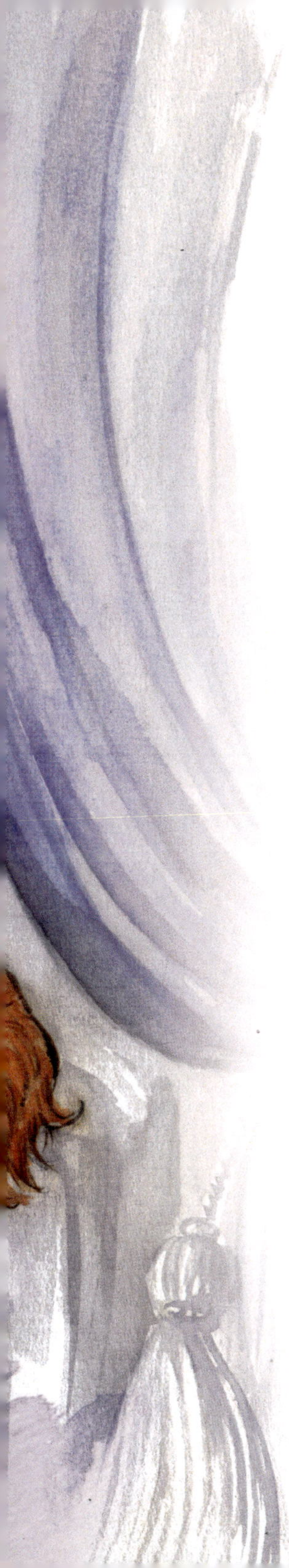

He remembered when he would play dead
oh, his body he would spread,
On the soft and cozy pillowcase
on the top of his MUM'S HEAD.

For he was older, by three I'm told
and by him the RULES were laid,
His sister's bed, it would unfold
was not where he would stay.

This would not do, **Bird** did ensue
her snores are like **THUNDER** to me,
Outside there is a **garden** here
could she not sleep up a **TREE?**

But **Pinky's redhead** will is strong
a not so easy one to break,
To be a good doggie girl I do not long
now **Bird's bikkies** I must **TAKE!**

There's a method to my sneaky plan
when there is CHICKEN,
PORK AND STEAK.
In order to get the food I love
good manners are forsake.

But I digress, let's put to rest
what Pinky really got,
Was a finger wag and a scold
it's outside you now must TROTT.

Down by the home where they did roam
to the **beach** they all did run,
Where **boats and yachts** swayed on the foam
and other puppies having **FUN.**

Pinky did find along the way
squirrels to her delight,
So off she went in a flash of red
they scampered away in FRIGHT.

But wait! Mum sang along the bay
you cannot catch the prey,
For local life should live in peace
and by Bird's side you now must STAY.

By water's edge they found some hounds,
Bird was a friend to all,
Into the water Pinky did flee
I won't come back if you CALL!

Bird had the knack to just stand back
and wet his furry paws,
To sharks I am a **juicy snack**
I don't wish to end up in those **JAWS!**

In Birdy's face to his disgrace
Pinky pushed her little butt,
To his dismay and surprised face
what a cheeky little MUTT!

For his little sis he did care
tho' her manners were but naught,
Next naughty thing you do, you know
you'll be sorry you were CAUGHT.

But **Pinky** with care not in the world
felt she was in her **prime,**
Pinky loved a little mischief
and she loved a little **CRIME.**

Bird had enough and knew he must
take the devil by the horns,
And knew in wisdom he could trust
from STRIFE she could be torn.

So gently showing her the way
his example made her think,
Happiness is to **share and play**
fire is red, but you are **PINK!**

Made in the USA
Las Vegas, NV
11 August 2023

75924796R00021